Helga Bansch has been illustrating children's books since 2003. Since then she has published over forty books and received dozens of prizes and awards, including the City of Vienna's Children's Book Prize for three consecutive years. She lives in Austria. Visit her website at www.helga-bansch.com.

First published in the United States in 2016 by
Eerdmans Books for Young Readers,
an imprint of Wm. B. Eerdmans Publishing Co.
2140 Oak Industrial Dr. NE
Grand Rapids, Michigan 49505
P.O. Box 163, Cambridge CB3 9PU U.K.

www.eerdmans.com/youngreaders

Originally published in Austria in 2013 under the title
In der Nacht
by Tyrolia-Verlag, Innsbruck-Vienna, Austria

Text and illustration © 2013 Helga Bansch
© 2013 Tyrolia-Verlag
English-language translation © 2016 Eerdmans Books for Young Readers

Manufactured at Tien Wah Press in Malaysia.

22 21 20 19 18 17 16   9 8 7 6 5 4 3 2 1

ISBN 978-0-8028-5471-1

A catalog listing is available from the Library of Congress.

The display type was set in Lino Stamp.
The text type was set in Helvetica.

FSC
www.fsc.org
MIX
Paper from
responsible sources
FSC® C012700

Helga Bansch

EERDMANS BOOKS FOR YOUNG READERS

GRAND RAPIDS, MICHIGAN / CAMBRIDGE, U.K.

At night, the elephant lies in
the tall grass,

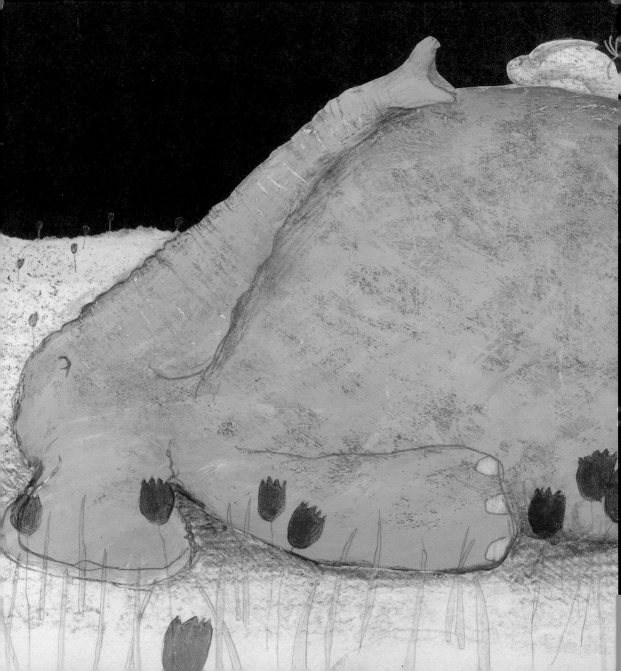

the bird dreams in her airy nest,

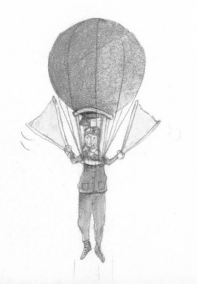

and the cat purrs behind
the warm stove.

The bat dangles from
the cave roof,

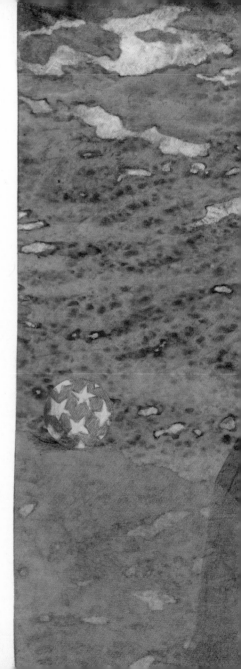

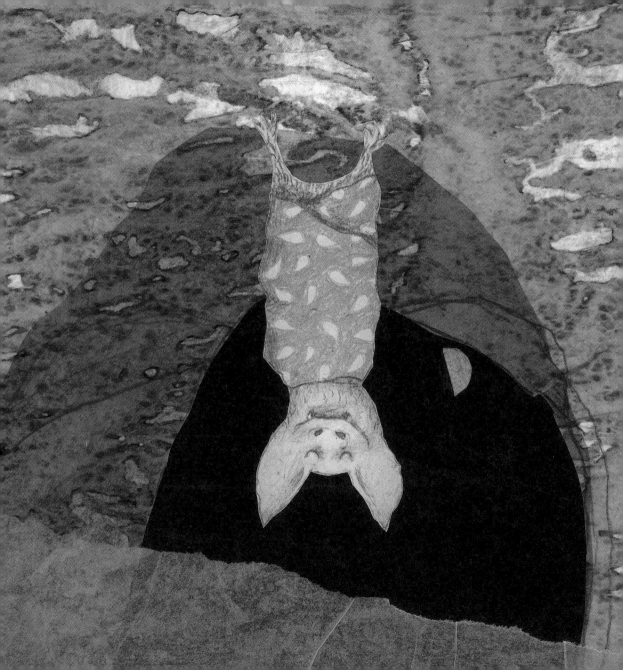

the rabbit lies in his burrow
on a cuddly cushion of hay,

and the leopard dozes
on a branch.

The dog slumbers in his cozy doghouse,

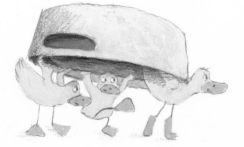

and the polar bear snores loudly
in his ice cave.

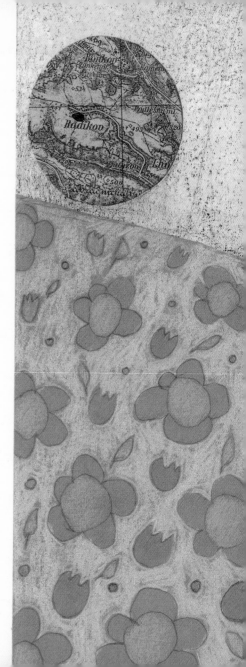

At night, Manu sleeps peacefully
in his bed.

And some nights Manu sleeps on a cloud, and dreams of chocolate and raspberry ice cream.

and the leopard dozes in
the ice cave.

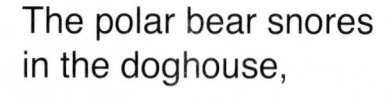

The polar bear snores
in the doghouse,

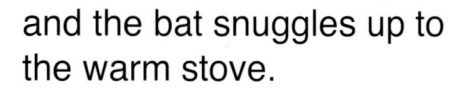

and the bat snuggles up to
the warm stove.

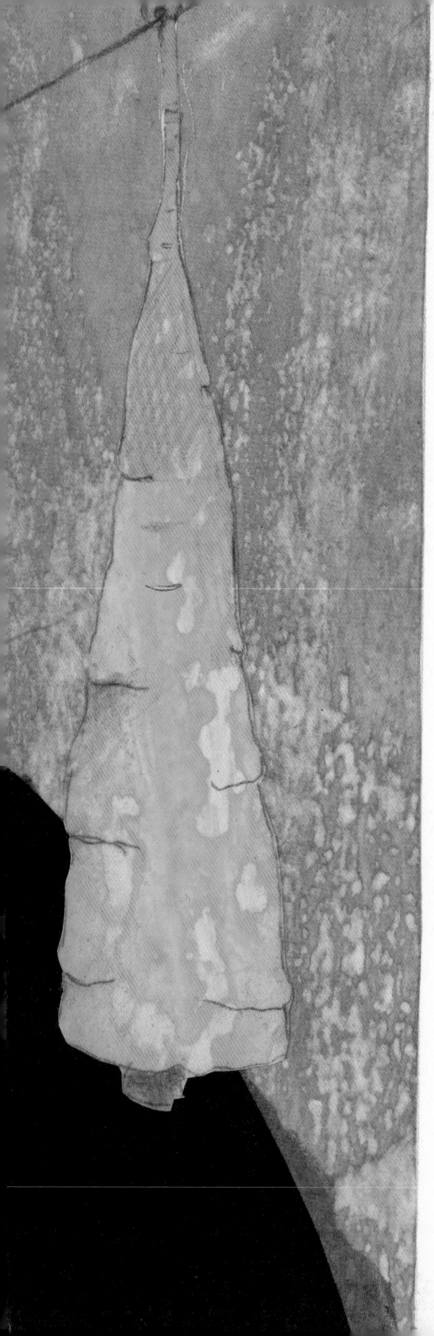

the rabbit dangles from
the cave roof,

The dog dozes on a tree branch,

and the bird lies in
the tall grass.

the cat purrs in a burrow
on a cushion of hay,

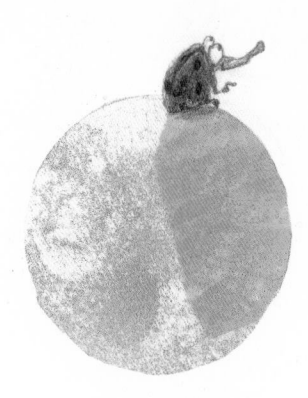

But sometimes at night the elephant
dreams in the bird's nest,

Helga Bansch

...but
At Night
sometimes

EERDMANS BOOKS FOR YOUNG READERS

GRAND RAPIDS, MICHIGAN / CAMBRIDGE, U.K.